PAUL IAN CROSS

SUPER QUESTERS

MISSION: RIVER CREST RESCUE

ILLUSTRATED BY
KATIE KEAR AND
CHERIE ZAMAZING

QuestFriendz

Written by: Paul Ian Cross
Illustrated by: Katie Kear and Cherie Zamazing
Edited by: Karen Ball, Speckled Pen
Designed and art directed by: Arvind Shah
STEM expertise by: Dr Thomas Bernard
Educational consultancy by: Diana Monteiro Toombs

1 3 5 7 9 10 8 6 4 2

This product is made of material from well-managed forests and
other controlled sources. The manufacturing processes conform to the
environmental regulations of the country of origin.
Printed and bound in Great Britain in February 2025 by
Clays Ltd, Elcograf S.p.A.

MIX
Paper | Supporting
responsible forestry
FSC® C018072
FSC
www.fsc.org

CONTENTS

RIVER CREST

SUNNY CREEK

CLOUD

MEADOW

HONEY GARDENS

WELCOME TO
SUPERQUESTERS

Join us on our new adventure, *Mission: River Crest Rescue*.
Strap yourself in for a problem-solving adventure that's full
of STEM (Science, Technology, Engineering, Maths). There are
puzzles to solve and codes to crack. Plus, science experiments
and a village to save. But we can't do it without you. Fire up your
mind and help us. *Thank goodness! You're here just in time...*

LEO (LEO ZOOM): Leo is obsessed with facts and figures and anything to do with space. Ask him a random question and he'll probably know the answer! His clear thinking, creativity and patience make him excellent at coding and maths. All these skills also make him great at coming up with solutions.

LILLI (LILLICORN): Lilli is known best for three things – her ability to take charge, her love of solving problems and her sense of curiosity. She really loves the natural world, everything from larks to llamas! She was born to explore – which makes her the perfect person to go on an adventure with.

BEA (BEA BUMBLE): Bea's superpower is her brain! It always buzzes with new ideas, and this makes her a born inventor. If you need something built, come to Bea. Her creative thinking makes her the perfect coding partner for Leo. Most of all, she's a loyal friend... which helps in sticky situations.

Chapter 1

The Science Shed

Picker's Patch hummed with life. A woman in a sunhat carefully planted seedlings. Beside her, a tall man pruned bushes with a set of shears. Bumblebees buzzed through the air, furry bodies bobbing. Dragonflies fluttered between lily pads on the pond, wings catching the sunlight like stained glass.

Outside the gate, Lilli and Leo met with a fist bump.

'Hey, Spaceman,' Lilli said, adjusting her ponytail so it rested on her shoulder. 'Why did you want to meet here?'

'Hey, Lil. Mum has a cold.' Leo nodded at the gate. 'How about we do her gardening tasks for the day?'

Lilli's face lit up. 'Yes! Bea can help too.' She paused. 'Hold on – where is Bea?'

Immediately, a breathless voice called out, 'Wait for me!'

They turned to see their friend jogging towards them, cheeks flushed.

'Hey!' Lilli cried. 'We wondered where you were!'

Bea placed her hands on her knees to catch her breath. 'Sorry...alarm...didn't...go off.' She straightened up. 'What's the plan?'

Leo updated Bea on the gardening mission.

'Count me in!' said Bea. 'I've been itching to get my hands dirty.'

The three friends passed through the gate, laughing together.

The woman in the sunhat looked up and waved. 'Hello, Leo! Where's your mum today?'

'In bed with a cold,' he said. 'We've come to help.'

She nodded. 'Well, let me know if you need anything.' This is what Leo loved about Picker's Patch. Everyone was always so kind and friendly.

'Oh, look!' said Lilli, pointing to a burst of colour along the path. Petals unfurled in shades of crimson and orange.

Bea crouched down, examining a row of small green pods. 'The beans are coming along nicely,' she said. 'They'll be ready for picking soon.'

The buzz of bees grew louder as they arrived at the hives – a cluster of white boxes on stands. Honeybees darted in and out like tiny, furry arrows.

'One, two, three, four...' Bea shook her head. 'Too many to count!'

'Did you know that bees fly faster than a chicken can run?' Leo said.

Lilli rolled her eyes. 'Random!'

Leo laughed. 'I learned it in a list of animals' speeds.' Leo was obsessed with facts and figures and anything to do with science.

They followed the path – left! right! – until they arrived at their allotment to find a sea of green vegetables, with splashes of colours from drooping daisies and sprawling sweet peas.

'Woah,' said Bea. 'Looks like we have our work cut out.'

'Mum always says that nature waits for no one,' Leo said, glancing around. 'Time to get going!'

Lilli tipped back her head to take in the towering sunflowers. Their golden petals glowed in the morning light. She pointed at the sunflower heads. 'How do they do that...I mean, how do they follow the sun?'

Leo's face lit up. 'Sunflowers turn their heads by growing more on the east side of the stem during the day, tilting the flower west as the sun moves across the sky. At night, the west side of the stem grows a little more, tilting the flower back east by sunrise.'

'Following the sun's path,' Lilli said.

'It's called heliotropism,' Bea added. 'By following the sun, they warm up faster, to attract more pollinators. And more pollination means...'

'More sunflowers!' Lilli cried.

Leo stretched onto his tiptoes and carefully gripped the head of a sunflower. 'Check this out,' he said. 'See how the seeds are arranged inside?'

The three friends leaned in close to look at the intricate spiral pattern.

'Beautiful,' said Lilli. 'They're overlapping. Like a jigsaw puzzle.'

'It's called the Fibonacci sequence,' Leo explained. 'A special mathematical pattern. It allows the sunflower to pack in as many seeds as possible.'

'Time to water the plants.' Lilli took a watering can, then frowned as trickles of water leaked out of the sides. 'Oh dear,' she groaned. 'It's broken.'

'We need to get another one,' Leo said. He glanced at his mum's shed and then hesitated. 'Maybe from...?' He pointed.

Lilli and Bea followed the line of his finger towards the wooden shed. It leaned wonkily to one side.

Leo's mum called it the Science Shed. It was where she experimented with new seedlings and kept all her gardening equipment – such as watering cans.

Leo absolutely, under no circumstances, was allowed to enter.

Never.

Not at all.

Ever.

But Leo's mum wasn't here today, and they only needed one watering can. Leo, Lilli and Bea nodded in agreement.

They went over and eased open the door, releasing a puff of musty air. Cobwebs shimmered in the sunlight that streamed through the grimy windows.

'Did you know,' Leo began, 'that a spider's web is five times stronger than steel? And spiders weave their webs in—'

'Orbs!' Lilli said. 'Threads that act as a scaffold. And then others in a spiral. It's called structural engineering, Leo!'

As their eyes adjusted to the dim light, they spotted tools hanging on hooks at the far wall, a lawn mower parked in front of them.

Bea gasped, moving towards a shelf of jars. 'Look at these!' Tiny green shoots poked through soil. Beside the jars there was a worn

notebook. She flicked through the pages.

'It's an experiment about light and plant growth,' she cried. 'This is like a science lab!'

Leo wandered to the bench. 'Check this out!' he called.

A tiny forest of delicate cress sprouts grew from a tray lined with damp paper. Beside it, celery stalks stood in glasses filled with water dyed different colours – red, blue, green. 'Mum's studying water absorption! She always has a science scrapbook. We should conduct our own experiments!' said Leo.

Lilli had already found something else to fascinate her. 'Hey, what's this?' she said, pointing to a contraption with a nozzle attached to a can.

'Some type of watering device?' said Leo.

'Just what we need,' said Lilli. 'Mission accomplished! Let's go.'

But before they had a chance to leave the Science Shed, their attention was drawn to something even more interesting: a large, ornate trunk tucked away beneath a bench.

All three of them walked over, as if drawn by magnets. Brass fittings gleamed above a heavy padlock.

'I wonder what's inside,' Bea whispered.

Lilli's eyes lit up. 'A mystery!'

Leo's mind raced. 'What does Mum have in there?'

Lilli spotted a dusty, old key on top of the bench. 'You'll need this,' she said, passing it to Leo.

Leo slipped the key into the trunk's lock and the lid creaked open.

'Wow,' Lilli breathed, glancing inside. 'It's like a time capsule!'

Faded maps lay beside leather-bound

notebooks. There were smooth pebbles, seashells and the spiral shapes of ammonites – fossils of sea creatures from another time.

Bea picked up one of the ammonites. 'This must be at least 65 million years old. Wow! That's 6.5 million times older than us!'

But it was a colourful box that caught Leo's attention.

His face lit up. 'No way! Questland!' He pulled out a board game. 'I used to play this when I was little. I thought it was lost! What's it doing here?'

They cleared a space on the floor and unfolded the game. Large, ornate letters were written across in gold ink: QUESTLAND.

On the board, there was a winding path that snaked its way through a breathtaking landscape. There was a green meadow bordered by lush forests dotted with towns and castles and a few golden spaces that looked like deserts. Everything was surrounded by a vibrant blue ocean.

'Look at these,' Lilli said, sifting through a small purple velvet bag. She pulled out three figurines, each painted with intricate details.

'I'll have the bee,' Bea said with a grin.

'I'll take the rocket,' said Leo.

Lilli held up the last piece – a griffin. 'This one is mine, then.'

One by one, they placed their markers on the 'Start' square.

'And now we need to put the pyramid in the centre of the board to begin the game,' Leo said, remembering the game's rules. But the box was empty.

'Hold on,' said Lilli. She rummaged through the trunk again. 'Found it!' Carefully, she

placed the glass pyramid on the square.

As Lilli took her hand away, a beam
of sunlight broke through the window.
Suddenly, the shed was filled with dancing
rainbows and sparks of light.

'Woah!' Lilli gasped. 'Is the game
supposed to do that?'

'I don't remember that from the rules,'
said Leo. 'Wait...what?'

Bea let out a startled squeak as her feet
left the floor.

'Guys, are you feeling this?' Leo asked, his voice quivering.

They looked at each other, wide-eyed and breathless, as they hovered above the worn floorboards. The air shimmered in all the colours of the rainbow. Then, the shed faded away in a cloud of sparkles as they flew up out of the roof and into the air.

'Goodbye, Picker's Patch!' Leo called.

With a final flash of light, the gardens disappeared, and they felt themselves whoosh through the air.

The friends all cried out at the same time. 'We're going...on an adventure!'

Chapter 2

A Magical Welcome

As the sparkles faded away, Bea, Leo and Lilli found their feet gently coming to rest on soft grass.

'Where are we?' Bea gasped.

They turned round in slow circles, taking everything in. They were standing in a meadow, dotted with colourful flowers and surrounded by trees. The air shimmered, filled with buzzing insects and there was a distant sound of rushing water.

And then came another noise. Munching.

The friends turned and froze to the spot.

'Are you seeing what I'm seeing?' Lilli
whispered.

'I see it,' said Bea, nodding furiously. 'I
can't believe it, but I see it.'

In the heart of the meadow stood a
creature straight out of a legend. Its golden
plumes gleamed brighter
than sunlight. The
feathers of an
eagle blended
into a lion's
body.
Massive
wings folded
at its sides.

'A griffin!'

Lilli gasped. 'A real-life griffin!'

With each twitch of its head, tiny embers flickered as if the animal was made of fire.

The griffin's gaze met theirs, eyes twinkling as if to say, 'Yes, I'm a real-life griffin.'

Then, with a toss of its head, the creature galloped away, leaving behind a trail of sparkles. It was heading towards the sound of water.

'Come on! Let's follow,' Leo cried. All three of them set off, running to chase it.

But when they arrived beside a stream, there was no sign of the griffin. Instead, three wobbly reflections stared back at them from the water.

'What in the world?' Leo cried, pointing. 'Look at us!'

They all wore brand new outfits!

Bea twirled around on tiptoes. 'I'm a bee!'

she cried. She sported a black and yellow striped bodysuit complete with delicate, translucent wings on her back. Between her two side buns bobbed a pair of springy antennae.

Leo wore a silver spacesuit and moon boots. 'I'm an astronaut!' he cried. He'd always wanted to be a space explorer.

Finally, Lilli was dressed in a shimmering suit that changed colour with every movement. She felt her eyes sparkle, along with her new outfit. 'This is amazing,' she said.

They noticed something else, too. Each of them wore an amulet around their neck. They were miniature replicas of their game figurines back in the Science Shed.

'Did the game bring us here?' Lilli asked.

'Maybe,' Leo said. 'Though I don't remember this ever happening before.'

Bea pointed at his forehead. 'What are those?'

Leo felt around and pulled off a pair of high-tech goggles. He noticed that the words 'Fact Finder' were etched on the side in glowing blue letters. The friends crowded round as he touched a big black button on the side. Information began to scroll across the lenses.

'Quick, put them on!' Lilli said.

Leo slipped the goggles over his eyes. He read the words out loud.

'WELCOME TO RIVER CREST, SUPERQUESTERS!'

'SuperQuesters?' Bea repeated, looking down at her bumblebee outfit. 'Is that...us?'

Suddenly, Leo's goggles lit up with a new message.

'SUPERQUESTERS, ASSEMBLE!'

he read aloud. 'Wait...there's more.

'LILLICORN, LEO ZOOM AND BEA BUMBLE.'

The friends exchanged startled glances.

'Lillicorn? Is that my mission code name? said Lillicorn, her amulet glinting in the sunlight. 'I love it!'

'Mine sounds like a real space hero,' Leo Zoom said, grinning.

'And mine feels right too,' said Bea Bumble, her wings fluttering with excitement.

'Hold on. Let's see what else we can

find out.' Leo adjusted his goggles as they whirred softly, looking for facts to share. 'OK,' he said. 'New information incoming.' Facts scrolled past his eyes. 'We're in QuestLand!' he said. 'It looks as if we've been transported into the board game.'

'Woah,' said Bea Bumble.

'Down there is a village', Leo Zoom added. He pointed to a gently sloping hill. 'Look, over there! It's a village fête.'

'I LOVE village fêtes!' Lillicorn cried, clapping her hands together.

Just then, the sun emerged from behind a fluffy cloud and their amulets began to glow with a warm, pulsing light. A bright rainbow arced across the sky, even though it wasn't raining.

Suddenly, Leo Zoom's goggles gave a sharp beep. Red text flashed across his vision. 'Uh oh,' he murmured. 'We have an enormous problem!'

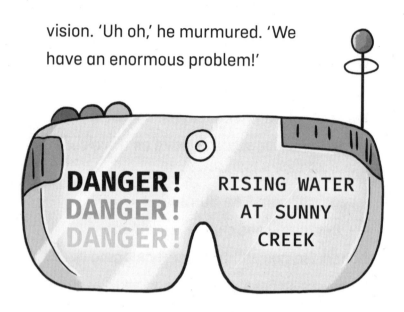

DANGER!
DANGER!
DANGER!

RISING WATER
AT SUNNY
CREEK

'Rising water?' Lillicorn repeated. 'But it's not even raining. And where's Sunny Creek?'

Bea Bumble's wings fluttered as she thought hard. 'Maybe this stream feeds into it? If we follow it, we could find Sunny Creek.'

Leo Zoom planted his fists on his hips.

'Exactly! And then we investigate. We're the SuperQuesters, after all! Maybe this is why the game brought us here. Let's check it out!'

They followed the stream down the hill, where the sounds of the village fête grew louder. Colourful tents dotted the edge of a meadow, and people wore all sorts of costumes, calling to each other and laughing. Games and stalls lined the paths and the aromas from waffle cones wafted through the air.

'Oh my,' said Lillicorn. 'I could do with an ice cream right now!'

As they drew closer, a tinkling laugh sounded to one side of them. When they looked over, a small figure hovered in the air nearby, her wings shimmering in the afternoon sun. A fairy!

'Hello there!' the fairy called out. Her emerald dress looked as if it was made of four-leaf clovers, petals overlapping. 'I'm Clover. Would you like to join our game of skittles?'

'Well, we're kind of on a mission...' Leo Zoom began.

Clover's eyes lit up. 'I love missions! What is it?'

But before Leo could answer, Bea Bumble cried out.

'Look!' She pointed towards the edge of the meadow. Water was slowly creeping up the slope, puddles forming in the grass.

Clover's wings fluttered. 'Oh no, Cloud Meadow! Is the water coming from Sunny Creek? It's never flooded before!'

'We need to get to Sunny Creek right

away,' Leo Zoom said. 'Do you know a quick way to get there?'

Clover's little fairy cheeks flushed with two pink spots of excitement. 'I do!'

Chapter 3

Beaver Bother

Clover led the way down a winding path, the sound of rushing water growing louder with every step. As they emerged from a thicket of bushes, Sunny Creek came into view – but it was far from sunny.

Leo Zoom's goggles whirred into focus as he took in the scene. 'Oh no! This is terrible. There's a flood.'

Lillicorn splashed through a puddle of water. 'And the meadow's turning into a swamp.'

'Hey! Look at me!' Bea Bumble cried. She hovered above the ground, her wings keeping her just high enough to stay dry. 'I can fly!' She fluttered above the group and did a somersault.

Clover gasped, pointing towards the creek. 'But what's causing this?'

Bea Bumble was higher now and had an excellent view. 'Look! Over there.'

Large furry shapes moved along the water's edge. One of the creatures slapped its flat tail against the water's surface.

Smack!

'Beavers!' Clover cried.

Leo Zoom used his Fact Finder goggles to take a closer look.

FUN FACT

Did you know that beavers' teeth continuously grow throughout their lives? Their daily activities mean they keep trimming them down, especially by grinding their teeth on wood such as tree bark!

'They're building a dam.'

'Let's get closer!' Bea Bumble zipped off towards the dam. Clover followed in the air, while Leo Zoom and Lillicorn ran along the water's edge. As they approached, they could see several beavers hard at work.

But something was wrong.

The dam was a messy pile of sticks and mud.

Bea Bumble hovered, examining the dam from above. 'This isn't right at all,' she said.

'Beavers are usually masters of natural engineering. This dam is a complete mess!' Bea loved inventing and building – which meant she totally understood how a beaver dam should be built!

'What do you mean?' Leo Zoom asked.

'Well, a beaver dam should be a careful combination of materials and techniques.' Bea Bumble glanced around. 'But everything here is piled up randomly. It's as if they made it in a rush.'

'I see what you mean,' said Clover, hovering beside her. Clover looked at Leo Zoom. 'It's much easier to see it from here,' she said and sprinkled some fairy dust over Leo Zoom and Lillicorn. Immediately, they began to lift off the riverbank.

'Woah!' said Leo Zoom, as he floated above the river. 'This is epic!'

Bea Bumble pointed out the different parts of the dam. 'See over there? They should be using logs and branches for the basic structure, carefully placing them to create a strong foundation. Then, they'd usually pack mud into the gaps to create a watertight seal. But this dam is full of holes!'

Lillicorn nodded. 'And don't forget about their lodges,' she said. 'Beavers use mud to build their homes like the way humans build walls with plaster. They construct a dam, stopping some of the water to form a pond. The pond is where they build their lodges, all safe and protected. Everyone needs a cosy place to sleep!'

'It's called engineering,' Leo Zoom added. 'It's—' But before he could finish, a dragonfly bumped into his nose. 'Woah,

woah, WOAH!' He'd lost his balance in the air and splashed down into the creek.

'Are you OK?' asked Clover.

'I'm fine,' Leo Zoom said, sploshing around. So much for being a superhero!

'Is it deep?' Lillicorn asked.

'Not at all,' Leo Zoom said, standing up to his knees in the water. He looked down at his outfit. 'I'm not wet at all. Cool! Our outfits are waterproof!'

Lillicorn was still thinking about the beaver dams, starting to work out what had happened. 'If the dams aren't being built properly, that's why they are flooding Cloud Meadow.'

Bea Bumble nodded. 'Exactly. But the question is, why aren't the beavers doing what they normally would?'

'That's what we need to work out,' Lillicorn said. 'And maybe help them do their jobs properly.'

Clover's wings shimmered with excitement. 'Well, SuperQuesters, it looks like you have found your mission!' She raised a hand in the air. Each of them ran over to give her a tiny high five. Fairy high fives were the best ever!

'We need to help rebuild the dam,' said Leo Zoom. 'This one is never going to work.'

Bea Bumble instantly took charge. 'OK, SuperQuesters! We need to redo this dam the right way.' She buzzed from place to place, pointing out changes. 'Let's start by laying a foundation made of logs and rocks. Then, we'll use medium branches – here, here and here – to create a criss-cross pattern. That'll give us stability.'

Stability meant strength.

Stability meant durability.

Stability meant that River Crest could be saved!

Bea Bumble and Lillicorn came down to land on the grass, then waded into the water. They began to work, rearranging the logs and branches, along with rocks and pebbles. They dug down into the creek bed to scoop up handfuls of mud to plaster everything in place.

Lillicorn helped to position some of the

larger branches. Leo Zoom used his Fact Finder goggles to examine how the water was flowing.

'It's getting better!' he cried, pointing to a puddle in the grass as it shrank down to a tiny dot.

Clover fluttered about trying to spot any tiny gaps the others might have missed. 'Team effort!' she cried.

Before long, they stood back and wiped the mud from their hands. The new dam stood big and strong.

Leo Zoom grinned. 'Great job, SuperQuesters. I'd say our mission was a success!'

'We did it!' Bea Bumble's wings buzzed with excitement.

But then...

Lillicorn pointed up the river. 'Look, the

beavers are there now!' They were working on a new dam, one that sent fresh water towards Cloud Meadow.

'But why are they undoing all of our hard work?' asked Bea Bumble.

Suddenly, one of the beavers started to slap its tail against the water, sending out tiny waves.

'What's going on?' asked Clover.

Next, another beaver did the same.

And then another.

All of them began to smack their tails against the water, louder and louder. They all stared at the creek's other bank.

'Are they trying to tell us something?' asked Leo Zoom.

Lillicorn's eyes lit up. 'I remember this. I watched a video about it online. When they slap their tails, they're either playing or they're warning for danger.'

Then, there was a piercing scream.

Clover fluttered to get a closer look. She gasped. 'Oh no! We have company. It's Mortifer!'

The SuperQuesters followed her gaze

to see a person standing by the river. He was dressed in dark green leggings, torn in several places. A ragged tunic hung off his body and a green hat perched on his head. He looked like a very scruffy goblin.

'Who's Mortifer?'

Bea Bumble asked, her antennae twitching.

Clover's face darkened. 'He's the goblin gardener. He's always hated River Crest because everyone is so happy here.'

Leo Zoom studied Mortifer through his Fact Finder goggles. 'I'm picking up some strange readings from his tool belt. It's emitting some kind of...bad energy? Yikes! He saw me!'

'Does he have anything to do with the beavers?' Lillicorn asked.

Before Clover could reply, Mortifer began dancing around on the spot. It was clearly not with happiness but in anger. He pointed a trembling finger at them. 'Get away! GET AWAY!' Then, in a rustle of leaves, he darted off into the trees.

Clover shook her head. 'Whenever

Mortifer's around, trouble is always close behind.'

Lillicorn felt a frown crease her brow. 'I think we need to have a word with Mortifer.' She didn't need Leo Zoom's Fact Finder goggles to understand that this goblin was behind the village being flooded.

Leo Zoom took a deep breath. 'SuperQuesters, we have a new mission.' He pointed after Mortifer. 'Follow that goblin!'

Chapter 4

The Maze Mystery

Clover led the way, her wings a blur of colour as she flew across a weathered wooden bridge. A sign beside it read, 'Sleepy Bridge'.

They had no time to be sleepy now!

The SuperQuesters raced across and stumbled to a halt as trees towered above them. The branches reached out like fingers and the leaves cast a deep shadow.

Clover whispered, 'These are called the

Talking Trees. They use the planet's energy to send out messages.'

'Good messages or bad messages?' Bea Bumble asked, her voice trembling.

'It depends...' Clover said, grinning, '...on whether you're a good or bad person.'

'Let me see if I can hear anything,' said Bea Bumble. She closed her eyes tightly and took a deep breath. Then she wrapped her arms around the nearest Talking Tree and leaned her ear against the trunk.

'She's having a

tree hug,' Lillicorn whispered to Leo Zoom.

Suddenly they were bathed in light.

Bea Bumble's eyes snapped open. 'The tree talked to me!' she cried. 'It told me which way to go.'

She led the group deeper into the woods. The forest around them turned darker. Tall spruces grew close together to form dense, green walls around narrow paths that twisted and turned. Then they arrived at an entrance.

'It's a maze!' Lillicorn cried.

Leo Zoom pulled on his Fact Finder goggles and scanned the structure. Using the goggles' heat-mapping technology, he spotted a short blob rushing down the paths. 'Mortifer is in there. He must use the maze to keep other people out.'

'Time to go after him,' said Lillicorn.

Leo Zoom squared his shoulders. 'Well, SuperQuesters, looks like we have a maze to solve and a goblin to catch! Are we ready?'

Lillicorn nodded. 'Born ready!' she said.

Bea Bumble's wings buzzed with anticipation. 'Let's do this!'

With Clover hovering above them, Bea Bumble entered the maze, ready to be guided by the whispers of the Talking Trees. But once they stepped inside, the voices disappeared. They needed to find a new way through the

maze. Bea Bumble stopped, her antennae twitching. She placed her hand gently on the leafy wall beside her.

'I've got it!' she cried, eyes lighting up. 'If we keep one hand on any side of the maze, we'll find our way to the centre. It's a classic maze-solving technique!'

Following Bea Bumble, the SuperQuesters wound their way through the green labyrinth.

FUN FACT

Do you know the 'hand on the wall' maze-solving technique? Enter the maze, place your right hand on the wall to your right, and follow it without letting go. Keep your hand sliding along as you walk, and you'll eventually find the exit!

Test the 'hand on the wall' technique for yourself on the maze map on page 5! Trace the right-hand wall with your finger from the entrance until you reach the centre.

Sunlight dappled the path before them.

They twisted and turned.

They turned and twisted.

Bea Bumble always had her right hand on one wall of the maze until...they found the heart of it!

In the clearing, there was a large shed. It wasn't like the Science Shed, but it was definitely a shed.

'What in Questland is that doing there?' Lillicorn asked. 'Why is a shed here?'

'Unless it wants to be hidden,' Leo Zoom said.

Clover fluttered closer to Bea Bumble. 'I don't like the look of this,' she whispered.

The SuperQuesters crept forwards, their footsteps muffled by moss. Was this where Mortifer was hiding?

There was a weathered sign nailed to the door:

'Not a friendly welcome,' said Leo Zoom.

'How rude!' Clover agreed with a frown.

But one feature stood out – a sleek modern tablet mounted next to the door. Its screen glowed with a set of numbers.

Bea Bumble reached for the door handle, but it didn't budge. 'Locked.'

'A locked door and a mysterious number pad,' said Lillicorn. 'This has to be a puzzle!'

Leo Zoom nodded. 'There's definitely a code to crack.'

The SuperQuesters huddled together, examining the tablet. Lillicorn frowned. 'The instructions say we need to input three numbers in the correct order to unlock the door...'

'Right,' said Bea Bumble. 'The only problem is, it could be any combination of numbers. We don't have much time. We have to get inside that shed!'

The friends looked around, searching for a clue. Suddenly, Leo Zoom grinned and put his goggles on.

'It might not work, but there's a chance my goggles can detect some hidden clues,' he said. After a couple of seconds, Leo Zoom let out a whoop. 'Yes! There's something coming up on the screen... OK

SuperQuesters, we have three sets of numbers and three clues.'

'Now we're talking!' said Lillicorn, giving both her friends a high five. 'Read them out, Leo, and we'll put our heads together to solve this in no time.'

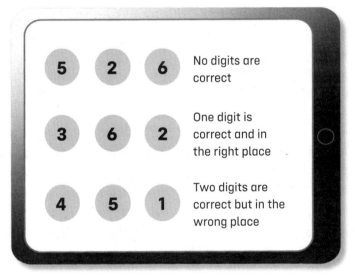

5 2 6   No digits are correct

3 6 2   One digit is correct and in the right place

4 5 1   Two digits are correct but in the wrong place

Leo Zoom read out the clues. Bea Bumble frowned, deep in thought.

'So, from the first clue we know that

all the digits are wrong,' Bea Bumble said. 'There's no five, two or six in the code. Which means... The correct digit in the second clue has to be three!'

'There are two correct digits in the third clue, but we know it can't be five, so four and one must be the right ones,' said Leo Zoom, grinning widely.

'Right, but four and one were in the wrong place. From the second clue we know that three is in the right place,' reasoned Lillicorn. 'So that means the code must be three, one, four!'

Bea Bumble tapped the code on the screen. After a second's pause, the screen flashed green.

SECRET CODE

3 1 4

Green for go! Gears started to turn and the door creaked open to reveal...the Shadow Shed!

Chapter 5

Dragonfly Disaster

'I'll go first,' Clover said, her voice strong and determined.

As she entered the gloom, something magical happened. Her wings began to emit a soft glow, illuminating the space with a gentle blue-green light.

'Wow!' Leo Zoom exclaimed. 'Your wings! They're glowing now. Did you know?'

Clover looked back over her shoulder. 'Oh! I forgot they could do that,' she said.

'All fairies have it. It's called bioluminescence – it's how fireflies light up too! I guess it comes in handy sometimes.'

As Clover lit up the shed, a sound caught their attention.

'Mortifer!' Lillicorn cried, pointing. A pair of green legs scrambled through a hatch in the shed's back wall. 'He's escaped!'

Bea Bumble ran after him, but the hatch slammed shut. 'He's got away!' she yelped.

Leo Zoom glanced around the shed. 'Well, at least we can investigate now.'

Lillicorn found a switch. She clicked it on and the room was flooded by an eerie green light.

The Shadow Shed was much bigger on the

inside than it appeared from the outside. Strange machines hummed and blinked. The walls were plastered with drawings for gadgets and lists of numbers.

'This is pretty high-tech,' said Bea Bumble, her antennae twitching.

'And these numbers look like binary code, a computer code that tells machines what to do,' said Leo Zoom, running a finger down a piece of paper taped to the wall. 'They're all ones and zeros and binary code only uses those two numbers!'

Metal cabinets lined the walls. Bea Bumble opened one of the doors to find it full of motor units, arms, pincers and paddles.

'These must be machine parts,' she said.

In another corner they discovered an assembly line, littered with half-built...

'Robots,' Bea Bumble whispered.

'Check out this one,' said Clover, hovering near a device with large, mechanical wings. 'It looks like a dragonfly. But why does Mortifer need to build a dragonfly robot?'

Leo Zoom's Fact Finder goggles beeped.

'PROBLEM...FLOOD...MEADOW!'

He let out a gasp. 'We have a BIG problem! I think Cloud Meadow is flooding even more. The fête is turning into a swamp.'

Clover's wings began to flutter with nerves. 'Oh no,' she whimpered. 'The fairies' home is in Shimmerleaf Oak. Petal Door is near the base of the

tree. So if the meadow's flooding...'

'Your home could be underwater!' Bea Bumble finished.

'We have to go back and warn the fairies,' Lillicorn said. 'Now!'

'Lead the way, Clover!' said Leo Zoom.

The SuperQuesters raced out of the Shadow Shed, following Clover as she fluttered ahead. They rushed out of the maze, past the Talking Trees, over the bridge and back to Cloud Meadow, where they stumbled to a halt.

Much of Cloud Meadow had turned into a lake. Stalls from the fête had fallen over and the ice cream van was up to its tyres in water. At one edge of the meadow stood Shimmerleaf Oak, branches reaching out. The water was getting closer and closer to Clover's home!

'We still have time,' Lillicorn said. 'Come on.'

The friends splashed over towards the tree. There was a little entrance in the tree trunk with a sign that read: 'Petal Door'.

Behind it was, the fairies' home!

Bea Bumble reached out to a tiny gold handle and opened the door for Clover, who flew inside. The friends leaned their ears against the tree trunk to listen.

Clover's voice rang out. 'Sorrel! Flora! Poppy! Come quickly. Cloud Meadow is flooding.'

She called more and more names and suddenly a cloud of fairies rose up into the sky, shouting out their thanks.

Clover was the last one to appear. 'My friends will be safe now. Thank you.'

As Bea Bumble watched the last fairy settle on a branch up above, she saw something else. 'Look!' she cried, pointing at the sky.

A mechanical shape darted towards them, its transparent wings catching the sunlight. It hovered for a moment before darting ahead of them, its long body unmistakable.

'It's a dragonfly drone!' said Lillicorn, her eyes widening. 'Just like the one we

saw in Mortifer's
workshop.'

'And not just
one,' Leo Zoom
said.

As they
watched, more
dots appeared on the
horizon. They grew bigger
and bigger.

'What is a group of dragonflies called?'
Leo Zoom asked grimly.

'A swarm,' Bea Bumble
said. There wasn't
just one dragonfly
drone – there
were too many
for the friends
to count.

They watched as the first drone led the way in a wide circle around the village. Then there was a whirring sound and a metallic door slid open in its belly.

A cloud of tiny black dots scattered down over the fields.

'It looks like pepper,' Bea Bumble said. Her dad loved to grind pepper onto his pizza – urgh. 'But that can't be right.'

Leo Zoom pulled on his Fact Finder goggles to take a closer look. 'No, they're seeds!' His goggles beeped a warning and flashed red. 'Evil seeds.'

The words had barely left his mouth when shoots burst out of the ground, growing taller by the second as they curled and snaked into the air. It was like watching a video in fast motion.

Clover gasped. 'That's Doom Sprout!'

she said. 'But I've never seen it grow this fast before.'

The plants continued to shoot up, their thick stems and leaves unfurling. Black vines snaked across the meadow, choking any flowers and covering the grass. Within minutes, a dense wall of vegetation had formed around the village.

'We're trapped!' Leo Zoom cried. 'Mortifer is trying to cut off River Crest

from the rest of Questland.'

Lillicorn couldn't believe her eyes – even the River Crest road sign was completely hidden now. 'But why would someone do this? It doesn't make sense.'

Clover clenched her tiny fists. 'I bet Mortifer wants River Crest for himself. Then he can take away all the happiness!'

Leo Zoom felt a horrible prickle of understanding. 'And if he takes over River

Crest, he could do the same with other places in Questland.' They hadn't been here long, but the friends could already see how special the kingdom was. Fiercely, he shook his head. 'We can't let this happen! We have to stop him.'

'But how? We don't even know where he is,' Lillicorn said, as her chin sank to her chest. Then she looked back up, a smile on her face. 'We need to go through this logically, step by step. Think back to where this all started – the river.' Lillicorn's mind whirred. She loved solving problems!

'The beavers were flooding the village with their dam,' Bea Bumble said. 'Beavers or...'

Lillicorn could almost read her friend's mind! They were working as a team. 'If Mortifer can make dragonfly drones, I bet he can also build beaver bots. Those beavers are flooding the meadow because he programmed them to do it.'

Bea Bumble grinned. 'You're right! They're robots. I remember seeing some pieces shaped like paddles in the cabinet.'

Leo Zoom clicked his fingers. 'Beaver tails! For beaver bots!'

Lillicorn turned to the flooded river. 'SuperQuesters! Time for action! We have a village to save!'

Chapter 6

Operation Doom Sprout

The SuperQuesters raced back to the river.
Clover flew through the sky above their
heads. On the bank, they could see the
beaver bots still working hard. They were
building another dam, but it looked terrible –
a mess of sticks and twigs.

'Could we build our own robots to fight
back?' Leo Zoom said.

Bea Bumble shook her head. 'No time.'

'We could dismantle the beaver bots,' Clover said.

Bea Bumble pulled a face. 'That doesn't seem right. All that technology gone to waste.'

What else could they do?

Leo Zoom thought back to the binary code he'd seen in Mortifer's shed. The computer code. His eyes lit up. 'Wait, I've got it! What if we reprogrammed the robots? I could use my tablet to hack their systems and write a better code. One that instructs them to build a proper dam that directs water away from the meadow.'

'That's a brilliant idea!' Lillicorn cried.

Leo Zoom slid the tablet out of his backpack. 'OK,' he said, thinking out loud. 'First, we need to make sure the beaver bots use the right materials. Then, they need to follow the correct sequence to rebuild the dam properly.'

Lillicorn peered at the screen. 'How do you do that?'

Leo pointed to a series of symbols displayed on his screen. 'Each of these refers to a specific instruction.'

'Just like an algorithm,' said Lillicorn, nodding. 'So each instruction is linked to the symbol beside it.'

At that moment, the SuperQuesters' amulets began to glow. As they looked, the glowing grew brighter.

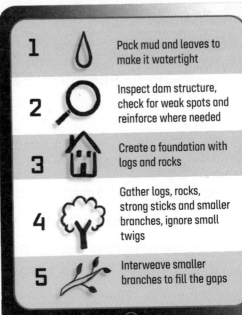

1. Pack mud and leaves to make it watertight

2. Inspect dam structure, check for weak spots and reinforce where needed

3. Create a foundation with logs and rocks

4. Gather logs, rocks, strong sticks and smaller branches, ignore small twigs

5. Interweave smaller branches to fill the gaps

Bea Bumble nervously reached for her amulet. Suddenly, the five coding symbols appeared in front of her, as if floating in mid-air like a hologram.

'What on earth?' said Bea Bumble in astonishment. She looked from the coding symbols in the air to Leo Zoom's tablet. 'Wait. Are these the same coding symbols you have on your tablet, Leo?'

Leo Zoom frowned. 'Yes...but they're in the wrong order.'

Bea Bumble reached out a hand towards the symbols. She touched the water drop symbol and dragged it down to the bottom of the order.

'Woah!' said Leo Zoom. 'It's like some sort of interactive hologram! This is so—'

'Incredible!' said Lillicorn.

'Phenomenal!' said Bea Bumble.

'Brilliant!' cried Leo Zoom. 'Lillicorn, press your amulet and see if it works too. I'll try mine.'

Each SuperQuester watched in awe as their interactive hologram hovered in mid-air.

'This is brilliant! We can work faster this way,' said Leo Zoom. 'Why don't we each have a go at rearranging the order?'

'Three heads are better than one,' said Lillicorn. 'Let's do it.'

Clover watched, biting her lip. Her wings beat furiously as the three friends concentrated on their task.

'OK, let's see what we've got so far,' suggested Bea Bumble.

'The first two steps in your program make sense, Leo, but I'm not sure you're inspecting the dam at the right time. I

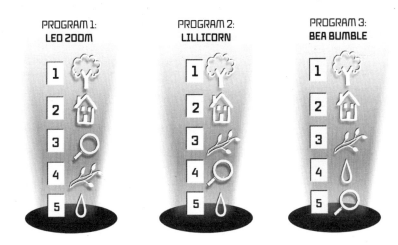

PROGRAM 1:
LEO ZOOM

1
2
3
4
5

PROGRAM 2:
LILLICORN

1
2
3
4
5

PROGRAM 3:
BEA BUMBLE

1
2
3
4
5

think it needs to come later in the sequence,'
said Lillicorn.

'Agreed,' said Bea Bumble, turning to look
at Lillicorn's sequence. 'The first steps in yours
look good too, Lillicorn, but I think the mud is
used too late.'

'I think Bea's right,' added Leo Zoom. 'I think
the mud needs to be plastered on the dam
before inspecting and reinforcing it.'

'Bea, let's take a look at yours,' said Lillicorn,
nodding to agree with her friends. They looked

carefully at the sequence and broad smiles spread across their faces.

'Excellent, Bea! This is it!' Lillicorn cheered, as Clover flew excitedly above their heads.

Leo Zoom followed Bea Bumble's sequence and carefully tapped the commands into his tablet. He held out the screen for Bea Bumble and Lillicorn to check.

'Now, let's see if it works!' Bea Bumble exclaimed as she hit the upload button.

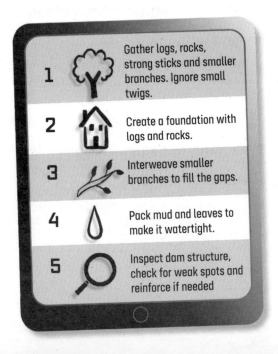

1	Gather logs, rocks, strong sticks and smaller branches. Ignore small twigs.
2	Create a foundation with logs and rocks.
3	Interweave smaller branches to fill the gaps.
4	Pack mud and leaves to make it watertight.
5	Inspect dam structure, check for weak spots and reinforce if needed

'Great teamwork, SuperQuesters!' Lillicorn said.

They watched the beavers. One by one, the creatures stopped what they were doing. Their eyes flashed red as they received Bea Bumble's new instructions.

Then the beavers blinked and their eyes went back to normal. They began to move away to another part of the river.

'Upload complete!' Leo Zoom said.

'Look!' cried Lillicorn. 'They're gathering new materials.'

The robots carefully sorted through logs and branches, selecting ones that looked big and strong. They began to construct a new dam. First, they cut the logs and branches to the right length using their long front teeth. Then they placed the logs along the river floor together with rocks to form a solid foundation.

'They're working in the right sequence,' Bea Bumble cried, her face shining with pride. 'The code is working.'

It wasn't long before the dam took shape, diverting water away from Cloud Meadow to flow downstream.

Lillicorn danced on the grass. 'You did it, Bea!'

But just then the dragonfly drones zoomed overhead with another storm of seeds! 'Bea, Leo? How many new computer programs can we write? We need to stop the Doom Sprout from spreading.'

They didn't need to be asked twice! They started again.

'Already on it! We can adapt the code for the dragonflies now.'

This time, they were able to work quicker. After a few adjustments, they waited for the dragonflies to come round again, then hit the upload button.

Just like the beavers, the dragonflies stopped and hovered in the air, bobbing up and down. Then their eyes flashed red, too.

'Uploading!' Clover cried, clapping her hands together.

Then the dragonflies moved off again. The friends all watched.

'What did you instruct them to do?' Lillicorn asked.

'Well, those metal wings look sharp,' Bea Bumble said. 'So first, we programmed them in a loop instructing them to look for Doom Sprout and then to cut down the black vines.'

'Genius!' Lillicorn said.

'Nope, just coding,' Leo Zoom laughed. He nodded towards the meadow. 'Let's go and see if it's worked. Every code needs a test.' That was how coding worked!

```
>

>

WHILE (KeepSearching == Yes):
  IF (Doom_Sprout IS found) THEN
      Cut(Black_Vines)
      KeepSearching = No
  ELSE
      KeepSearching = Yes
```

CANCEL   **UPLOAD**

All three of them ran to Shimmerleaf Oak. Clover followed in the air. Then they climbed up into the branches. The other fairies' laughter tinkled as Sorrel pointed. 'Look!'

They settled in a row on a branch and gazed over Cloud Meadow. They had the perfect view. The water was beginning to drain away, but there was a tall, giant barrier of writhing stems around the edge of the village.

Doom Sprout.

Leo Zoom pointed at some little dots flying through the sky. 'The dragonfly drones are on their way.'

The dragonflies drew closer to the Doom Sprout. What would they do? Drop more seeds or rescue the village? One by one, the dragonflies began to descend through the air.

'They're doing it!' Leo Zoom whispered. 'They're actually doing it.'

The dragonflies flew lower and lower before plunging into the Doom Sprout. Their wings were flashes of silver amongst the black vines.

Bea Bumble began to explain. 'Dragonflies are the athletes of the natural world,' she said. 'They can perform all sorts of acrobatics! And their four wings allow

them to fly carefully.'

'And trim carefully, too,' Lillicorn said.
Sure enough, the Doom Sprout was
collapsing as the dragonflies flew in a
formation between the stems. It was like
watching a set of dominoes falling over!

'Operation Doom Sprout is a go!'

As the Doom Sprout fell to the ground, it shrivelled away to nothing and the cottages came into view again. One by one, front doors opened and villagers stepped out.

A crowd formed at the edge of Cloud Meadow, cheering and waving as the last of the Doom Sprout fell in a pile.

'What next?' Lillicorn asked, rubbing her hands together.

The dragonfly drones had come to hover in the air beside Shimmerleaf Oak. It was almost as if they were waiting for some new instructions.

Clover's eyes lit up. 'I have an idea!' She flew over to Leo Zoom and whispered in his ear. His face split into a huge grin.

'Well?' Bea Bumble asked.

'How would you like to drop some new seed bombs? Ones that will help River Crest?' Leo Zoom asked. He turned to the fairies. 'But we'll need your help.'

Sorrel's, Poppy's and Flora's magical smiles filled the air with happiness.

Chapter 7

Magic Takes Root

The friends scrambled down as the fairies lined up in a row, wings fluttering.

'What do you want us to do?' Clover asked.

'We need seeds for bee-friendly flowers, wild flowers, herbs and vegetables,' Leo Zoom explained.

'Maybe also some water-loving plants to help prevent future flooding?' Lillicorn added.

The friends couldn't stop smiling. This was such a good plan! It would help them heal

River Crest, as well as rescue it.

'Let's make it happen!' Leo Zoom said.

The fairies each gave little salutes, then they started to fly between the wild plants, dipping their hands into flower heads or shaking them gently. They gathered the seeds in the pockets on their fairy dresses.

'Every good dress needs pockets. Look at that!' Bea Bumble counted the wild flowers. 'Cornflowers, poppies, foxglove and marigolds. We'll have all the seeds we need!'

Lillicorn grinned. 'The perfect meadow mix.'

As the fairies worked, Leo Zoom set to work on his tablet for one final time. 'Let's reprogram the dragonflies for a new mission – meadow magic.'

Bea Bumble and Lillicorn went to the river to collect handfuls of rich, damp soil.

'This soil is perfect,' Bea Bumble observed.

'Full of goodness. It will help our new plant friends thrive.' Because that was what they were doing now – planting new friends!

As they gathered up oak leaves bigger than their hands, the fairies flew over to join them. Bea Bumble and Lillicorn laid out the leaves in a row on a fallen tree trunk. They were like little package wrappings, waiting to be tied up. Then the fairies flew along the

row, leaving handfuls of seeds on top of each leaf. Lillicorn had rescued some long grasses and the friends used them to tie up the leaves in neat parcels.

'Perfect seed bombs!' Bea Bumble said, as they stood back to inspect their work.

It didn't take Leo Zoom long to upload the last piece of code. The dragonfly drones seemed eager to help. They hovered above each parcel and the friends got ready to tie their oak leaves to the dragonflies' tummies. But how?

'I know,' said Bea Bumble. 'Remember what we learned about spider webs back at Picker's Patch? They're strong.'

'Of course,' said Leo Zoom. 'We can use spider silk to create harnesses!'

The fairies went along the trees that lined the riverbank, collecting spider silk from abandoned webs. One spider crawled down from his web to see what was happening and was happy to offer his own silk.

Working carefully, they used strands of silk to secure the seed bombs to the drones.

Finally, everything was ready. Leo Zoom tapped his screen and the dragonfly drones took off into the air, flying across the meadow.

Lillicorn gasped. 'Look! The amulets are glowing again!'

Quickly, the three friends pressed their hands to their amulets. An interactive hologram appeared before them. This time it showed a map of Cloud Meadow in grid form, with all the locations visible.

'So, we need to make sure that the seed bombs are dropped at the Bee Hive, the Living Tree and the Gazebo,' said Leo Zoom, pointing them out on the map.

'But we should also try to make sure we find the shortest route possible,' Lillicorn said. 'I'm not sure how long the dragonfly drones will be able to keep going.'

'We should hurry,' agreed Bea Bumble. 'Let's each write a program and compare them at the end. Three heads are better than one, right?'

The SuperQuesters got out their notebooks and began writing their programs, determined to help Cloud Meadow flourish once more.

'How are you getting on?' asked Leo Zoom.

'Done!' shouted Lillicorn and Bea Bumble in unison.

They gathered around to look at each program in turn.

'Err, Bea...I think you made a mistake,' said Lillicorn.

'You seem to have mistaken the "Leaving

LEO ZOOM'S PROGRAM:
{3 x UP} + {1 x RIGHT} + {3 x UP} + {1 x RIGHT} + {6 x DOWN} + {4 x RIGHT} + {4 x UP}

BEA BUMBLE'S PROGRAM:
{1 x RIGHT} + {3 x UP} + {2 x RIGHT} + {1 x UP} + {3 x RIGHT}

LILLICORN'S PROGRAM:
{3 x UP} + {1 x RIGHT} + {3 x UP} + {5 x RIGHT} + {2 x DOWN}

tree" for the "Living tree",' said Leo Zoom.

'Oh,' said Bea Bumble laughing. 'Well, at least both of your programs are correct. But I think we should use Lillicorn's program.'

'You're right,' said Leo Zoom, comparing his program with Lillicorn's. 'Your program takes the shortest route, Lillicorn. My route has a total of 22 steps, but yours only has 14 steps.'

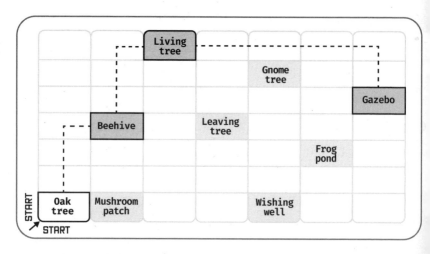

LILLICORN'S PROGRAM:
{3 x UP} + {1 x RIGHT} + {3 x UP} + {5 x RIGHT} + {2 x DOWN}

Leo Zoom tapped out the program quickly on the tablet, whilst Lillicorn and Bea Bumble checked his code for mistakes.

'Looks good, Leo Zoom,' said Bea Bumble.

'Fingers crossed this works!' Lillicorn said, as she tapped the upload button.

The friends waited nervously as they watched the dragonfly drones fly out across Cloud Meadow.

One by one, the new seed bombs fell from their bodies and burst open, bright seeds scattering in clouds.

'It's working!' Clover cried.

Before their eyes, new green shoots sprouted out of the soil. But these weren't Doom Sprout, but colourful petals that unfurled.

'Absolutely magical!' Bea Bumble gasped.

But only the amazing speed the plants grew was magical. Their solution of rewilding Cloud Meadow was science! They cheered as Cloud Meadow burst into a riot of colours. Soon, Petal Door was surrounded by all the shades of the rainbow.

'We did it!' said Lillicorn.

But then, Clover's tiny face scrunched up. 'Wait a minute,' she said. 'Some of these plants are going to need support. We can't just plant seeds and forget about them.'

Leo Zoom agreed. 'They'll need help, like in Picker's Patch. Remember all the structures we saw there?

Lillicorn nodded. 'Of course. We need trellises!'

The friends huddled together and began to make notes and sketches.

'We could take bamboo canes for the

main structure. They're light but strong.'

Bea Bumble's wings buzzed. 'We can use twine to create a criss-cross pattern between the canes. That would be perfect for the sweet peas to climb up!'

'Don't forget the runner beans,' Lillicorn added. 'They'll need something sturdy to wind around as they grow.'

Clover flittered about between them. 'The clematis will need to spread out,' she suggested.

Together, they designed a variety of structures. Some were tall and straight for the beans and peas, and others were fan-shaped. They even created some arches for the roses.

They found a stack of canes leaning against a wall, along with some twine to tie the poles together. They stuck canes in the ground and began to build their frames. All the time they worked, the plants were growing bigger and bigger and...they started to realise that maybe they couldn't do all of this by themselves.

'Can we help?' cried a voice. It was a man, carrying more canes. Other villagers were coming over, armed with rakes and spades. They were still wearing their costumes from the fête! Knights and princesses, pirates, clowns and fairies were all joining the friends to pitch in.

'They're fairy-tale gardeners!'

Lillicorn cried.

Soon, the garden was dotted with different people, all of them helping to clear the soil and erect the trellises. A man in a sunflower costume dug over the soil and a girl in a red cape drew neat rows in the ground.

Lillicorn laughed. 'I never thought I'd see a mermaid planting sweet peas!'

Bea Bumble buzzed beside her. 'It's like the most magical gardening party ever.' It made her whole body fizz with pleasure to see everyone working together.

Another villager arrived, carrying a tray of sandwiches. She went from group to group, handing them out. 'You must be starving,' she said, when she arrived beside the SuperQuesters. Bea Bumble felt her tummy rumble. They were! They each took a

handful of sandwiches.

'Is it just me,' Lillicorn asked, 'or do Questland sandwiches taste extra good?'

'Double extra good,' Leo Zoom agreed, taking a huge bite.

After a slug of fresh lemonade, they went back to work. Slowly, River Crest began to be transformed.

'All it takes,' Leo Zoom said, huffing and puffing with a spade. 'Is time, logic and patience. Gardening is just like coding!'

By the end of the afternoon, they'd put all the structures in place to support the growing plants that bloomed with colourful flowers. River Crest was full of nature. The villagers walked around the meadow, taking in all their hard work.

Clover fluttered in circles, her wings leaving trails of sparkles. 'It's more beautiful than I ever imagined,' she gasped.

As she spoke, Leo Zoom's Fact Finder goggles erupted in a series of urgent beeps.

Quickly, he pulled them on. 'It's Mortifer. He's back!'

Chapter 8

Mortifer Returns

A ragged figure raced across the meadow. He pushed villagers out of the way and began yanking canes out of the ground. Then he stamped on the flowers, crushing their new petals.

'No, no, NO!' Mortifer screamed. 'This isn't what I wanted at all!'

Clover's wings drooped. 'He's destroying everything we worked for.'

Lillicorn galloped over and planted herself in Mortifer's path. Leo Zoom came

up on one side while Bea Bumble cleverly crept round behind him. Clover hovered above.

Mortifer was surrounded.

'Why are you doing this?' Lillicorn asked him. 'Can't you see how beautiful River Crest is now?'

The goblin glared at Lillicorn, his chest heaving. 'Beautiful? It's ruined! River Crest was supposed to be mine. I was going to make it unhappy!' He looked around as if he couldn't believe what he saw. 'Now, it's a flower wonderland. Urgh, how disgusting!'

Lillicorn took a deep breath, forcing herself to be patient. After all, hadn't Leo Zoom said how important patience was? 'But can't you see?' she said. 'The villagers have done all this with teamwork. Why can't you be a friend to River Crest? It might make you happy.'

Mortifer narrowed his eyes, as if he was thinking. Had Lillicorn won him round? Then his expression hardened. 'Being happy makes me unhappy!'

He snatched up another cane, but it flew out of his hand and arced high over the meadow before crashing into a cluster of beehives near Honey Gardens.

'Oh dear,' Bea Bumble whispered. 'This isn't going to be good.'

There was a moment of silence.

And then...

A low buzz filled the air, growing louder by the second.

Suddenly a swarm of angry bees erupted from a hive, their buzzing now a roar.

Mortifer's eyes widened. 'Oh no!' he whimpered. 'I really don't like bees.'

The bees flew in a cloud of little bodies, headed straight for Mortifer. The cloud took the shape of an arrow slicing through the air.

Mortifer let out a shriek and took off, the

swarm in hot pursuit. He raced across Cloud Meadow and splashed through the river to disappear into the Talking Trees. He'd escaped – again!

But the SuperQuesters burst into cheers. 'Goodbye, Mortifer!' they cried. 'And good riddance.'

Leo Zoom grinned at his friends. 'I don't think that naughty goblin will bother River Crest again soon. Not now that he's made an enemy of the bees.'

By now, the sun was starting to set, casting a golden glow over the meadow. The SuperQuesters gathered together, with Clover flying in circles above their heads.

Lillicorn pulled back her shoulders. 'We couldn't have saved River Crest without teamwork. That's the real magic here – everyone coming together.'

As the sky filled with a brilliant orange of the setting sun, Cloud Meadow burst into a last flurry of activity. The villagers set up the fête again, righting stalls and setting out games. The air was filled with laughter and carnival music.

A jolly man dressed as a jester approached them, his bells jingling merrily. 'After everything you've done today, you're our guests of honour!'

He turned to a woman dressed as a teddy bear. 'Over here, quick! It's the SuperQuesters who saved River Crest.'

The crowd gathered around, chanting their name. 'SuperQuesters, SuperQuesters SUPERQUESTERS!'

As the friends wandered through the fête, they came across a stand selling lollipops.

'Oh, they look delicious,' Lillicorn said.

The stall holder, dressed as a butterfly, beamed at them. 'They're made from the wild blackberries that grow right here in the meadow,' she explained, handing each of them a lollipop. 'Nature's own sweet treats.'

Bea Bumble's eyes lit up. 'Healthy too. They're full of antioxidants and vitamins!'

'Even better,' said Lillicorn.

Next, they found themselves at the base of an enormous slide. Children in fairy wings and dragon tails whooshed down. Gleeful shrieks filled the air.

'Come on, let's have a go!' Leo Zoom said, scrambling up the ladder.

One by one, they zoomed down the slide, the wind rushing past them.

As they tumbled off the end, Lillicorn shook out her rainbow-coloured mane. 'That was amazing! The perfect combination of

gravity and centrifugal force.'

They wandered over to a coconut shy. The stall owner, dressed as a pirate, handed them three balls each. 'Give it yer best shot, me hearties!'

Leo Zoom took aim, his tongue poking out in concentration. With a mighty throw, he sent a coconut tumbling off its perch. 'Woo-hoo! I did it!'

'Do you know...' Lillicorn said, 'that the hard walls of a coconut shell can help humans make buildings to survive an earthquake?'

'I did know that,' said Leo Zoom, grinning.

Lillicorn beamed. 'Of course you did. You're a SuperQuester!'

Clover fluttered up to her new friends. 'You've done more than save River Crest,' she said. 'You've made a friend for life.' Her eyes welled up as she gave tiny fairy hugs to each of her friends.

'It was our pleasure,' said Bea Bumble.

The sun dipped lower, disappearing beneath the horizon. There was a final flash of sunlight that reflected off the amulets hanging around the friends' necks. The gems sparkled and pulsed with magical energy that warmed their bodies.

'Do you feel that?' asked Leo Zoom. 'I think it's time...'

Clover's mouth turned down. 'I don't want you to leave.'

'I promise we'll be back,' Lillicorn said. She felt it was true, deep in her tummy.

'Of course we will,' said Leo Zoom. 'There's no place we'd rather be!'

Clover zipped above them, leaving sparkles in her wake. 'Thank you,

SuperQuesters – for everything!' The fairy blew them each a tiny kiss. As the kisses travelled through the air and brushed against their cheeks, the world around them began to spin.

Whoosh!

It was time. The SuperQuesters were going home.

Chapter 9

Superhero Skills

In the blink of an eye, the three friends
landed back in Picker's Patch, surrounded
by the familiar scents of earth and flowers.
They looked down to find their SuperQuester
outfits...gone. They were back in their
normal clothes. Leo reached to check the
top of his head. His Fact Finder goggles had
disappeared.

Lilli didn't have her sparkling colourful
hair anymore and Bea's black and yellow

outfit was back to her jeans and T-shirt.

But their special amulets still hung around their necks.

Bea's eyes sparkled. 'We've discovered a portal to a whole other world!'

'A world full of magic and friends,' Lilli added, thinking of Clover.

'And amazing adventures!' said Leo. 'I can't wait until the next time.'

A familiar voice called from across the garden. They turned to see Leo's mum, her dungarees smudged with dirt.

'Hello, gang. Ready to go home?'

'Mum, you're better!' Leo cried.

'Yes. It was strange. I was so ill this morning, but then I felt completely fine. Like magic!'

The SuperQuesters shared a secret glance. They all knew about magic!

Leo's mum began to examine the trellises. 'Wow, you've been busy. Thank you for all this work.'

'It was our pleasure,' said Bea for the second time that day. 'We learned loads of new skills. Watering, digging, planting. Pretty standard day at the allotment really.'

'I'm so glad,' said Leo's mum.

Bea nodded. 'Oh yes, it's been quite educational!'

'Super educational,' added Lilli, barely able to contain her giggles.

As they gathered their things to leave, the amulets pressed against their chests, reminding them of their incredible journey. It had taught them so much – about engineering, coding, beavers, dragonflies, fairies...and friendship.

'You know,' Leo said. 'I have a feeling our SuperQuester days are only just beginning.'

Bea nodded. 'Absolutely. We have skills now – real superhero skills!'

'And we make a great team,' said Lilli.

Bea's and Lilli's parents had come to collect them too. As the friends parted ways at the gate, they shared one last knowing look.

The sun was setting here, just like in Questland, burning orange as it dipped below the horizon. It was a colourful end to an extraordinary day.

Bea, Lilli and Leo knew that nothing would ever be the same again. They were SuperQuesters now, and they felt certain that there were more adventures to come...

THE END

Glossary

Ammonites – a group of extinct sea creatures that lived before, and at the same time, as the dinosaurs.

Centrifugal force – a force that appears to make objects move outwards when they are spinning around something.

Code/coding – a set of step-by-step instructions that tell a computer what to do.

Fibonacci sequence – a series of numbers where each number is the sum of the two previous numbers (e.g. 0, 1, 1, 2, 3, 5, 8, 13, 21, 34).

Gravity – the invisible force that causes objects to move towards the ground.

Heliotropism – the movement of a plant in response to the direction and movement of the sun.

If/Then statements – statements that allow a computer to make a choice.

Seed bombs – small bundles, or balls, of clay, soil or compost filled with wildflower seeds.

Structural engineering – the use of mathematics and science to design structures (such as bridges or buildings) so that they can withstand forces without becoming damaged.

Trellis – a structure or framework that is used to help support climbing plants.

Water absorption – the process by which something takes in water.

SUPERQUESTERS

MORE INTERACTIVE STORIES

Puzzle-packed picture books

STEM learning for ages **4+**

100 reusable stickers and a reward chart

NEW ADVENTURES COMING SOON!

SCIENCE SAFETY

ALWAYS TAKE EXTRA CARE WHEN USING SHARP OR HOT OBJECTS AND NEVER PUT ANYTHING IN YOUR MOUTH. ALL ACTIVITIES AND EXPERIMENTS IN THIS BOOK SHOULD ONLY BE DONE WITH HELP FROM A GROWN-UP!

ACTIVITY 1: COLOURFUL CELERY

WHAT YOU NEED:

- A leafy celery stalk
- Dark food colouring (red or blue works best)
- Large cup
- Water
- Spoon

METHOD:

1. Fill the cup halfway with water.

2. Add at least 10–15 drops of food colouring to the water. Mix it using the spoon.

3. Cut off the bottom of the celery stalk so that it is nice and fresh.

4. Put the celery stalk in the water.

5. Wait 24 hours to see the results (Extra challenge – make a prediction and check on the experiment every 2–4 hours, noting down what you can observe!)

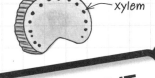
Xylem

HOW DOES IT WORK...?

Water moves upwards through plants, from the roots to the leaves, using small tubes called xylem. Xylem transport water and minerals upwards from the roots by a process of capillary action. Capillary action is the ability of a liquid to flow in narrow spaces without help from an outside force.

INVESTIGATE!

- What happens if more or fewer food colouring drops are used? Do the leaves change colour faster or slower?
- What about using different plants or flowers, such as ones with white petals?
- What happens if the bottom half of the stalk is split in two, and each half is placed in a glass with different food colouring?

ACTIVITY 2: BUILD A DAM

WHAT YOU NEED:

- A tin foil tray or watertight container
- Natural materials to build with — e.g. sticks, leaves, rocks
- Modelling clay (play-dough, plasticine or clay)
- Jug of water

METHOD:

1. Take a tin foil tray or container and begin building a dam in the middle of the tray, across the 'river'. Use modelling clay to help stick the natural materials together to build the dam and stop the water from flowing.

2. Once the dam is built, pour water into the tray to test it!

3. Don't worry if the dam doesn't work the first time. Look for any changes that can be made to improve the design and then test it again.

DID YOU KNOW...?

Beavers are one of nature's natural engineers! They build dams using a range of materials such as sticks, logs, rocks and plants, and use mud like glue to hold the dam together. Beavers use the pond that forms behind the dam to help protect them from predators, access food more easily, and build their home (called a lodge).

INVESTIGATE!

- What happens if rocks are placed at the bottom of the dam or if different materials are used?
- What materials are the best?

ACTIVITY 3: MAKE SEED BOMBS

WHAT YOU NEED:

- Native wildflower seeds or seeds collected from the garden
- Soil
- Flour
- Water
- Mixing bowl
- Tray

METHOD:

1. Mix one part flour to 10 parts soil.
2. Slowly add water and mix until it becomes sticky and dough-like.
3. Roll the dough into balls the size of golf balls.
4. Roll the mud balls in a tray filled with wildflower seeds until the balls are fully covered.
5. Leave the balls to dry for 24 hours until they have hardened.
6. Plant the seed bombs on a bare patch of garden/dirt by throwing them at the ground. Watch them grow!

DID YOU KNOW...?

Seed bombs are a great way to sow seeds in unreachable or neglected areas and they help provide food for wildlife. It's best to use seeds from native wildflower species as they're already adapted to the local climate and geology.

INVESTIGATE!

- What happens if different types of seeds are used? Which ones are most effective?
- Are seed bombs that have lots of seeds more successful than those with fewer?
- What happens when different areas are seed bombed? How do the conditions of different places affect the success of the seed bombs?
- Sow the wildflower seed bombs in pots and test which are the most successful!

ACTIVITY 4: MAKE A TRELLIS

WHAT YOU NEED:

- Small plant in a pot
- Wooden food skewers / wooden lolly sticks
- Twine
- Scissors
- Paper
- Pencil

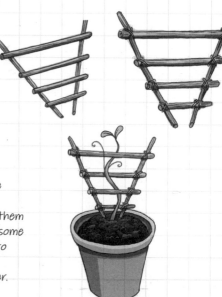

METHOD:

1. Start by planning and drawing the trellis design..
2. Gather the wooden sticks and lay them out in your planned shape. Leave some space at the base (at least 5cm) to insert into the plant pot.
3. Use twine to tie the sticks together. Ask an adult to help tie the knots tightly if needed.
4. When the trellis is complete, gently place it in the plant pot. Lift the plant leaves gently and tuck their tendrils into the twine.

HOW DOES IT WORK...?

A trellis is a simple structure that helps plants grow upwards! They can be made from many different materials and in different shapes. Trellises help plants get more sunlight, better air circulation and make it easier for pollinators to pollinate the area!

INVESTIGATE!

- What improvements could be made to your trellis? Is there a design shape that works better?
- What other materials could you use instead to build the trellis structure?
- Are some designs more effective for certain plants?